ME I

AM!

Jack Prelutsky

Pictures by Christine Davenier

SCHOLASTIC INC.
New York Toronto London Auckland
Sydney Mexico City New Delhi Hong Kong

ISBN 978-0-545-39762-9

Text copyright © 1983 by Jack Prelutsky.
Illustrations copyright © 2007 by Christine Davenier.
All rights reserved. Published by Scholastic Inc.,
557 Broadway, New York, NY 10012, by arrangement with
Farrar, Straus and Giroux, Inc. SCHOLASTIC and associated
logos are trademarks and/or registered trademarks of Scholastic Inc.

12 11 10 9 8 7 6 5 4 3 2 1   11 12 13 14 15 16/0

Printed in the U.S.A.   08

This edition first printing, September 2011

Designed by Barbara Grzeslo

"Me I Am!" originally appeared in *The Random House Book of Poetry
for Children*, New York: Random House, 1983. We are grateful to Jack
Prelutsky and Random House for granting us permission to use it in
this picture book.

In memory
of
Martha Alexander
—J.P.

To all the ME I AM's
who helped create this book,
with special thanks
to Melanie
—C.D.

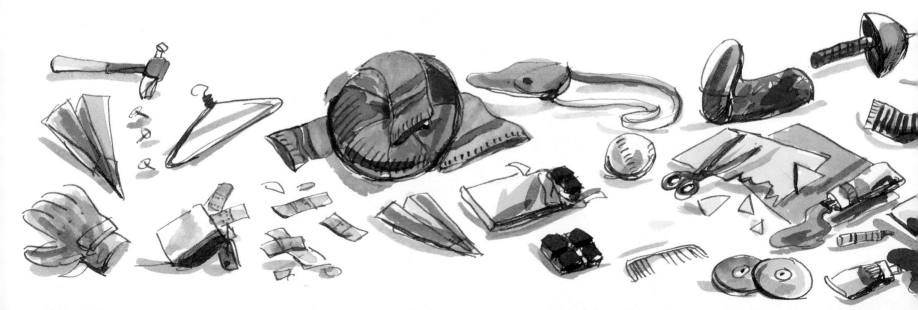

I am the only ME I AM
who qualifies as me;
no ME I AM has been before,
and none will ever be.

No other ME I AM can feel
the feelings I've within;

no other ME I AM can fit
precisely in my skin.

There is no other ME I AM

who thinks the thoughts I do;

the world contains one **ME I AM**,
there is no room for two.

I am the only ME I AM
who qualifies as me;
no ME I AM has been before,
and none will ever be.

No other ME I AM can feel
the feelings I've within;

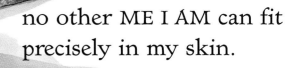

no other ME I AM can fit
precisely in my skin.

There is no other ME I AM

who thinks the thoughts I do;

the world contains one ME I AM,
there is no room for two.

I am the only ME I AM
who qualifies as me;
no ME I AM has been before,
and none will ever be.

No other ME I AM can feel

the feelings I've within;

no other ME I AM can fit

precisely in my skin.

There is no other ME I AM
who thinks the thoughts I do;

the world contains one ME I AM,
there is no room for two.

I am the only   I AM
this earth shall ever see;

that ME I AM I always am

is no one else but—

ME I AM!

I am the only ME I AM
who qualifies as me;
no ME I AM has been before,
and none will ever be.

No other ME I AM can feel
the feelings I've within;
no other ME I AM can fit
precisely in my skin.

There is no other ME I AM
who thinks the thoughts I do;
the world contains one ME I AM,
there is no room for two.

I am the only ME I AM
this earth shall ever see;
that ME I AM I always am
is no one else but ME!